OVER THE RIVER AND THROUGH THE WOODS

No part of this publication may be reproduced in whole or in part, or
stored in a retrieval system, or transmitted in any form or by any means,
electronic, mechanical, photocopying, recording, or otherwise, without
written permission of the publisher. For information regarding permission,
write to Scholastic Inc., 555 Broadway, New York, NY 10012.

ISBN 0-439-13658-X

Illustrations copyright © 1992 John Gurney.
All rights reserved. Published by Scholastic Inc.
CARTWHEEL BOOKS™ is a trademark of Scholastic Inc.

SCHOLASTIC and associated logos are trademarks
and/or registered trademarks of Scholastic Inc.

12 11 10 9 8 7 6 5 4 3 2 1   9/9 0 1 2 3 4/0

Printed in the U.S.A.   08
First Scholastic printing, October 1992

Over the River and Through the Woods

Illustrated by John Steven Gurney

SCHOLASTIC INC.
New York Toronto London Auckland Sydney
Mexico City New Delhi Hong Kong

I would like to thank Mom, Dad, Phyllis, Brian, Lauren, and Steven for posing; Linda Barclay and family for use of the sleigh; the Mercer Museum for their historical assistance; and Patty Anne, Brian, and Christopher for the cameo with the snowman.

To the warmth and comfort of Thanksgiving,
to my parents for providing it, and, as always,
to Kathie.

— J. S. G.

*O*ver the river and through the woods,
To Grandmother's house we go.

The horse knows the way
to carry the sleigh

Through the white and drifted snow.

Over the river and through the woods,
Oh, how the wind does blow!

*It stings the toes
and bites the nose,*

As over the ground we go.

Over the river and through the woods,
Trot fast, my dapple gray!

*Spring over the ground
like a hunting hound,
For this is Thanksgiving Day.*

Over the river and through the woods,
Now Grandfather's face I spy!

Hurrah for the fun!

Is the turkey done?

Hurrah for the pumpkin pie!

Over the River and Through the Woods

O - ver the riv - er and through the woods, To Grandmother's

house we go. The horse knows the way to car-ry the

sleigh Through the white and drift - ed sno - ow. O - ver the

riv - er and through the woods, Oh, how the wind does

blow! It stings the toes and bites the nose, as

o - ver the ground we go.